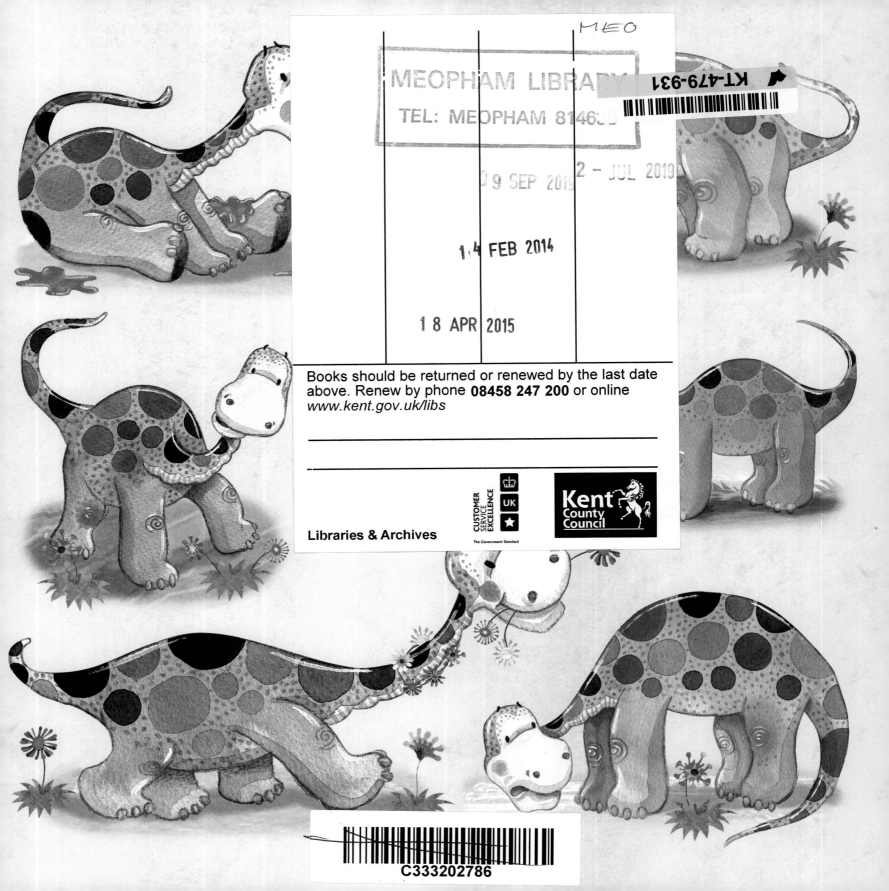

Emmy's
Eczema

First published in 2012 by Wayland
Text and illustrations copyright © Jack Hughes 2012

Wayland
338 Euston Road
London NW1 3BH

Wayland Australia
Level 17/207 Kent Street
Sydney, NSW 2000

Editor: Victoria Brooker
Design: Lisa Peacock and Steve Prosser

British Library Cataloguing in Publication Data
Hughes, Jack.

Emmy's eczema. -- (The dinosaur friends)
1. Eczema--Pictorial works--Juvenile fiction.
2. Children's stories--Pictorial works.
I. Title II. Series
823.9'2-dc23

ISBN 978 0 7502 7055 7

Printed in China

Wayland is a division of Hachette Children's Books,
an Hachette UK Company

www.hachette.co.uk

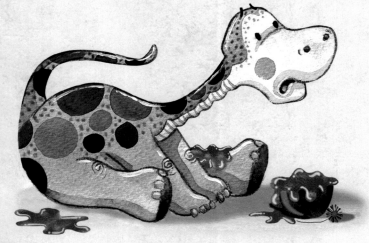

Emmy's Eczema

Written and illustrated by Jack Hughes

WAYLAND

Emmy has eczema.

This means that sometimes
her skin gets itchy and sore.

Emmy felt a little bit
shy about her eczema.
Occasionally her friends Rex,
Dachy and Steggie would
notice and ask questions.

"Does it hurt?" "Is it sore?"
"Can I touch it?" "Will I get eczema now?"
"Of course not, don't be silly," Emmy
would reply grumpily.

Emmy knew she should not scratch her skin when it felt itchy. Scratching only made her eczema worse.

SCRATCH! SCRATCH!

But sometimes it was
very hard to resist.

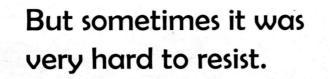

Emmy's mum made a special cream
out of flowers gathered from the Jurassic
meadow on the other side of the valley.

Sometimes Emmy complained. "Yuck! I don't like it. It's too sticky!" But the cream did soothe Emmy's eczema and stopped it itching.

One day, Emmy's mum had run out
of Emmy's special eczema cream.

So she sent Emmy and her friends off to gather flowers from the Jurassic meadow.

It would take a long time
to get there.

They would need to walk through the forest, cross the river and then climb the big hill. As they set off, Emmy noticed that her leg was starting to itch.

By the time they reached the forest Emmy was feeling very itchy. Emmy saw the rough bark of a large tree and before she could stop herself... SCRATCH...SCRATCH...SCRATCH...

SCRATCH!
SCRATCH!

Emmy rubbed her skin against the tree.
"No, Emmy! You MUST NOT SCRATCH!" shouted
Rex. But it was too late. Emmy's skin looked red.

When they reached the bank of the river Emmy felt really itchy. She saw a large rock and before she could stop herself...

SCRATCH!
SCRATCH!

SCRATCH...SCRATCH...SCRATCH...
Emmy rubbed her skin against the rock.
"NO, Emmy! You MUST NOT scratch!"
shouted Dachy. But it was too late,
Emmy's skin looked sore.

The friends walked upstream to find a shallow place to cross. Emmy's leg felt itchier than ever. Along the edge of the riverbank were large scratchy bushes with spiky red flowers. Emmy could not resist...

SCRATCH...SCRATCH...SCRATCH...
Emmy scratched her skin against the bushes.
"EMMY, NO! STOP SCRATCHING!" her friends
all shouted together. But it was too late. Emmy's
eczema looked very red and sore indeed.

As they crossed the river, the cold water soothed Emmy's sore leg.

But as they climbed the hill Emmy's leg became red and sore and itchy again. "Come on everyone, hurry up!" said Rex, "Emmy needs those flowers."

When they reached the top of the big hill, the Jurassic meadow was laid out below them like a brightly coloured carpet. "LET'S GO!" shouted Dachy. The friends rolled down the hill together and into the meadow.

Emmy, Rex, Dachy and Steggie landed, laughing, in a big heap at the bottom of the hill. They were surrounded by the most beautiful flowers.

The friends chased and played. Suddenly Emmy noticed something. "I don't feel itchy anymore!" she said with great relief. "It must be the flowers!" said Rex.

The friends had a wonderful time in the Jurassic meadow. Rex and Emmy gathered flowers to take home to Emmy's mum.

Steggie made beautiful garlands for them all to wear
and Dachy flew round and round chasing the butterflies.

By the time they headed home
Emmy's eczema felt much better.
Emmy decided she would try really
hard not to scratch her eczema again...

...and maybe her mum's eczema
cream wasn't too sticky after all!

Meet all the Dinosaur Friends - Steggie, Dachy, Rex and Emmy!

978 0 7502 7056 4

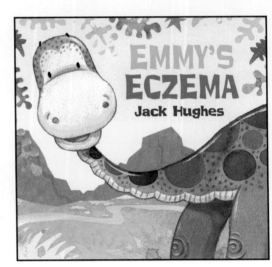

978 0 7502 7055 7

978 0 7502 7057 1

978 0 7502 7058 8